This Little Tiger book
belongs to:

For my big brother, Jonah.
Thanks for letting me share your flat
~ M P T

For Brian and Ivy, my lovely in-laws
~ A E

LITTLE TIGER PRESS
1 The Coda Centre, 189 Munster Road,
London SW6 6AW
www.littletiger.co.uk

First published in Great Britain 2014
This edition published 2015

Text by Maudie Powell-Tuck
Text copyright © Little Tiger Press 2014
Illustrations copyright © Alison Edgson 2014

Alison Edgson has asserted her right to be identified as the
illustrator of this work under the Copyright, Designs and Patents Act, 1988

A CIP catalogue record for this book is available from the British Library

Printed in China • LTP/1800/1145/0415

2 4 6 8 10 9 7 5 3 1

Pirates Aren't Scared of the Dark!

Maudie Powell-Tuck • Alison Edgson

LITTLE TIGER PRESS
London

"Look, Parrot!" cheered Freddie.
"I've painted a pirate flag!"
Freddie had built a pirate tent in the
garden and Mum was letting him sleep
in it all night long. He couldn't wait.

"Can I stay in your pirate tent tonight?"
asked his sister, Poppy, peeping in.
"No way!" Freddie snorted.
"Why not?" said Poppy.
"It will be spooky and there
will be scary sea monsters,"
said Freddie. "Pirates aren't
scared of the dark –
but fairies are!"

Freddie stomped off to play
by the paddling pool. He was
sinking a ship of evil penguins
when Poppy raced over.
"Fairy ahoy!" she cried.

SPLASH!

"Fairies are rubbish pirates," grumbled Freddie. "Leave me alone!" And he squelched back to the house to dry off.

But Poppy wouldn't go away. When Freddie got back to his tent, there she was!

"Look, we're having a pirate tea party," she said. "Please, please, please can I stay out with you tonight?"

"Pirates *hate* tea parties!" shouted Freddie. "This is *my* tent, *my* toys and *my* sleepover. No stupid fairies allowed!"

Poppy's wings drooped. With a sniff, she trudged away, dragging her wand behind her.

Outside, the sun dipped in the sky
and it grew dark. But Freddie
didn't mind one bit.

First, he made funny shadows
with his torch. Then he read
Parrot a scary story about a
giant squelchy octopus.

Suddenly . . .

flicker – flicker – pop!

. . . the torch went out!

"Pirates aren't scared of the dark," said Freddie with a shiver.

Rustle, rustle, rustle...

"Who's there?" Freddie squeaked.

Rustle, rustle...THUMP!

Something was inside the tent!

"It's the giant squelchy octopus!"
yelled Freddie.

"Oo-ar!" cried Poppy, leaping out.
"I'm Captain Fairydust and I've come
to steal your ship. Walk the plank
or I'll turn you into a frog!"

"You're no match for Captain Growlyboots," cheered Freddie, reaching for his sword.

He swished it through the air, then grabbed Poppy's wand. "Prepare to be froggified!" he cried.

But Poppy had gone quiet.

"Shh!" she whispered. "There's something outside."

Slowly, they peeped out into the shadowy garden.
Rustle, rustle, rustle. . .

A big, black shape was coming towards them.
"What if it's a pirate beastie?" trembled Poppy.
Rustle, rustle, rustle. . .

The thing was getting closer and closer.
"Hold my hand," whispered Freddie.
"We'll zap it with your wand.
One, two, three . . ."

"Monsters beware!" they yelled.
"Pirates aren't scared of
the dark!"

"Of course they're not," said Mum.
"But I've brought a special pirate
lantern just in case."
   "Pirates always sleep with a night
light," nodded Captain Growlyboots.

"Do pirates like midnight feasts too?"
smiled Mum.
   "Yes please!" said Captain Fairydust, and
they sipped cocoa under the twinkling stars
until it was well past a pirate's bedtime.

"Tell me a story," said Poppy as they snuggled into bed.

"Once," began Freddie, "there were two pirates."

"What were they called?" yawned Poppy.

"Captain Fairydust and Captain Growlyboots,"
said Freddie, "and they were the bravest
brother and sister to sail the seven seas."

   And the two little bears swapped
swashbuckling stories
until they both fell
fast asleep.

BOOKS ahoy!
More wonderful adventures for little pirates!

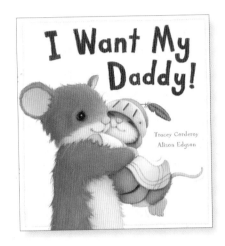

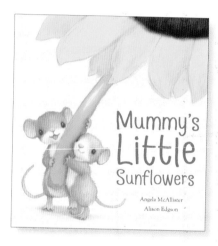

For information regarding any of the above titles
or for our catalogue, please contact us:
Little Tiger Press, 1 The Coda Centre,
189 Munster Road, London SW6 6AW
Tel: 020 7385 6333 • Fax: 020 7385 7333
E-mail: contact@littletiger.co.uk • www.littletiger.co.uk